TRULY DETERMINED

Written by Lynn Arren

Lynn loves to hear from her readers! You can contact her at contactlynnarren@gmail.com

CHAPTER 1: Back In Session

"Please take out your notebooks for the next problem." Mr. Abbot, our Calculus teacher, directed. The whole class opened their notebooks to blank pages and prepared to write the problem down.

"Let us take the function f(x) =4x^2 + 2x + 1. When x = 4, is the function increasing or decreasing? Is the function concave up, or concave down?" he wrote as he spoke.

The others got to work. I sat there, staring out the window, looking at the ocean. It was beautiful, as always. I vaguely felt the stares of some of the others on my back.

"Uh, Mr. A.?" Tristan asked. Tristan sat at the desk next to me. He was the class clown, known for his jokes and carefree attitude.

"Yes, Tristan?" Mr. Abbot responded with a hint of annoyance in his voice. He was quite used to Tristan interrupting.

"Can I hit up the restrooms? It was Taco Tuesday for lunch today.. And, well.. Let's just say, I don't think the guac was the freshest." He rubbed his stomach. The other students snickered.

"Certainly," Mr. Abbot said. Tristan got up, grabbed the hall pass hanging by the door, and headed out into the hallway. "How's everyone else doing with the problem?" he asked. Noone responded.

"Okay then.. I'll just assume you're all so smart you figured it out independently and on the first try!" he said sarcastically. The class smirked.

Mr. Abbot walked around glancing at our notebooks. He stopped when he reached my desk.

"Claire," he startled me, but I didn't jump. I simply looked up at him. "How's it going?" he asked.

How's it going? I thought about his question. How could I even answer it? Ever since Benjamin left me with no way to contact him, I had felt nothing but deep emptiness and depression. It was as if my heart was literally absent from my body.

"Fine," I lied. I turned back to stare out the window. I kept hoping, praying even, that I would spot the Serpent's Skull somewhere on the horizon. But so far, no such luck.

It had been five months since Jacquelyn, Camden, and I returned to Trenton after our nautical adventure aboard a ship full of pirates. Five *miserable* months. Five months of therapy: First individual, and then family, insisted upon by my father. Five months of me crying myself to sleep every single night. Five months of missing Benjamin with a passion and a desperation that I never even knew existed.

"Do you have a pencil?" Mr. Abbot asked, looking down at my blank paper. I had a pencil sitting right on my desk, easily visible to him. But, I knew what he meant. *Why hadn't I written anything down?*

"I do," I simply said, and reached for the pencil. I looked up at the board and quickly started to copy the problem. I actually used to enjoy math class, unlike history. I found it to be useful, for the most part.

"Well," he cleared his throat, "you let me know when you find the solution," he spoke as he walked back to the front of the room. It was nice of him to give me a break. Luckily, all my teachers had been pretty understanding about my lack of enthusiasm in school since returning. I could tell they felt bad for me. Nobody knew where I'd been or what I'd been up to. We'd done a good job of keeping the details a secret. We didn't want to be locked up in the loony bin, after all. Or worse - what if the authorities tried to find Benjamin? What if they charged him with kidnapping? Everyone just assumed that I'd gone through a very traumatic experience and that I didn't want to talk about. And that was fine by me.

Tristan returned from the bathroom, hanging the hall pass back on the wall and then heading to his seat. He peeked up at the board, and then glanced quickly over to my paper. "Pssst..." he whispered. "What's the answer?"

I looked at him, expressionless. I hadn't solved the problem; I'd only written it down so Abbot would leave me alone. I shrugged. Tristan groaned.

Mr. Abbot spent the remainder of the class going over how to solve the problem. When the bell rang, he reminded us about an assignment due tomorrow and to bring in canned goods for the food drive the sophomore class was sponsoring.

I quickly gathered my things and headed towards the door. My next stop was my last class of the day: History with Mr. Harper. I had become surprisingly more interested in history after my experience with Benjamin and his crew. Having lived with people who were actually born in the 1800s had been such an authentic learning experience about the past. But oh, how I missed him...

In history, Mr. Harper had us finishing up a unit entitled *History of Our Community*. Basically, each student had to research information about Trenton and its surrounding areas, type up a report, and then present the information to the class. Harper was big on presentations. Luckily, he nor the school required Jacquelyn and I to make up any of the work that we missed when we were gone. They had called it "extenuating circumstances". It was a good thing, because there was no way to make up three months' worth of classwork *and* homework before graduation in June. And I was hellbent on graduating and getting out of there.

The people in Trenton were curious, that much was obvious. You should have seen the way they looked at Camden, Jacquelyn, and I each morning as we walked into school. They thought that we were freaks; Freaks who disappeared with no good reason and no believable explanation. The police were more forgiving. They asked a lot of questions, but insisted that the three of us had been through a very traumatic event and probably blocked out a lot of memories. *Sure*, I thought, *we'll go with that*. But there was no way to forget *him*, and I was determined not to.

The bell rang just as I was daydreaming about Benjamin waiting for me on the pier. I imagined what I would do; what I would say to him. I wondered what he would have been up to these past few months. I was so angry that he left me the way that he did, but the anger quickly dissipated as I thought about being able to kiss him just one more time...

Maybe I'm the one who's cursed, I thought to myself. *After all, first I lost Camden. That was horrible. Now I finally have Camden back, but I've lost Benjamin. It's like I'm destined to lose everyone I love.* Now that I really did believe in curses, the thought sent shivers down my spine.

CHAPTER 2: Will You?

I grabbed my things and headed to my locker. I just needed to grab my calculator and math book before meeting up with Jacquelyn and heading home for the day.

"Hey," said the confident voice of a man to my left. I closed my locker and looked to see David Wiles, the star of our high school's basketball team. I used to have a crush on David, back before I met Benjamin. I would have melted if he'd randomly stopped to chat with me then. Now, however, I found him to be a bit immature and average looking. Probably because Benjamin was *so* handsome...

"What's up?" I replied, as cheerfully as I could. I gave a small smile and then waited. His eyes were watching me curiously. He seemed just a tad bit nervous.

"I was wondering if you had plans after school today," he said. I detected a little uncertainty. He looked down at the floor and then back to me.

"I'm sorry," I lied, "I'm super busy today." I didn't feel like hanging out with anyone. I didn't feel like doing anything. Still, it was unusual for David to even *ask* me to hang out. We hadn't really talked much since last year. I don't think we spoke at all since I returned from my adventure on the sea. "Why do you ask?"

"Oh, um," he started, stuttering slightly. "I just.. Well.. Are you planning on going to prom this year?" he blurted out. His face was bright red.

"Prom?" I asked. I had totally forgotten about the Senior Prom. What month was that again? May? *Oh crap*, I thought, *it's May already!*

"Yeah.. did you have a date already?" He was visibly nervous and sweating a bit around his hairline. Was David Wiles trying to ask me to the prom? Nine months ago, this would have been a dream come true. But now, it didn't feel like anything. I felt absolutely no emotion whatsoever.

"Oh," I started, "I don't know if I'm going yet," I simply said and started walking. I thought maybe he would fall behind. I could walk fast.

"Well, do you want to go with me? As my date?" he asked, hurrying to keep up. I stopped and looked at him. *How funny is time? I thought. I literally would have done anything for this exact moment not too long ago... and now, I don't think I could have cared any less.*

"Oh, um... Let me just check some things first," I replied. "I'll get back to you," I nodded in assurance as I quickly stepped down the steps of Trenton High School and ran to meet Jaquelyn under the old oak tree.

"Sounds good!" he yelled as I ran off. His face was a mix of bewilderment and relief. I wondered what he thought I was going to say. I had the feeling that he wasn't all that used to girls not being interested in him.

"How was your day?" Jacquelyn asked as she gave me a huge hug. She looked like a supermodel waiting there for me.

"Same as usual," I replied nonchalantly. "You?" I gave her a smile. I knew if I told her that David had just asked me to the prom, she would turn it into a huge deal. I didn't really have any desire to go to the prom with him, or to even go to the prom at all. So, I kept my mouth shut.

"It was good, actually. You'll never guess who asked me to the prom! Jon Daeton!" she squealed and kicked up her back leg. It looked like a typical cheerleader move.

"Seriously?" I asked. "That's awesome. Congrats!" and I hugged her again. "When did he ask you?" I wondered if Jon and David had planned it so that we were both asked to prom on the same day. They were best friends, after all.

"Just today!" she shrieked. "I'm in total shock. I bought a dress just in case, but nobody had asked me and I didn't really want to go solo..." she started. She bit her lip and looked down. I could tell that she was happy, but she felt bad for me. She knew that if I could go to the dance with anyone in the entire world, it would be Benjamin, and I would probably never see him again. I was so grateful that Jacquelyn was able to understand me when nobody else ever could.

"Well I'm super happy for you," I said, squeezing her hand. We walked home slowly, stopping to pick up Camden on our way.

CHAPTER 3: Shopping Is
A Girl's Best Friend

"Do you think I should wear red?" Jacquelyn asked. "It's kind of flashy.. I don't know. Too much?" She held up a red mermaid style dress with lots of sequins.

"It's flashy, but I feel like that's you," I told her honestly. We had been shopping for prom dresses for two hours. The prom was a week away, but luckily, Jacquelyn had the perfect figure, so she'd be able to fit in something right off the rack.

"I don't know.. I do like the red. But maybe I try pink? It's softer," she mulled it over. There were hundreds of dresses in the tiny formal dress shop in Trenton called *Très*

Paris. Everything was crammed into such a small space, you really had to dig through racks and racks of dresses in order to feel like you'd looked at everything.

"Pink is nice," I replied simply. I lifted up the price tag for one of the dresses. Three hundred dollars and change. Was this place for real? "Jeez, these are pricey!" I whispered. The most I'd ever paid for a fancy dress was $60, and it was to wear to a relative's wedding.

"I know, but they're the best quality. And they're each one-of-a-kind. The owner gets them shipped in from a designer in Europe." Leave it to Jacquelyn to know all of the details. She had quite a few brand-name dresses hanging in her walk-in closet.

I walked around, softly touching the dresses. The silky ones felt nice on my fingertips. I stopped when I reached a velvet navy blue dress. It reminded me of Benjamin's overcoat.

Jacquelyn saw me looking at it. "That would look amazing on you, Claire!" she insisted. "Why don't you try it on?"

"That's alright," I shook my head. I knew the second I put it on, I wouldn't be able to stop thinking about him. "I don't think I'm going to the prom." I declared.

"What do you mean.. You don't *think* you're going?" Jacquelyn looked confused. "So, you *might* come?" she asked excitedly. "Claire! You *should* come! It will be fun! It will be nice for you to get out of the house for a change."

I never told Jacquelyn that David Wiles had asked me to go to the prom with him last week. I had avoided David like the plague, even walking outside and back into school through different entrances to get to my classes so that I didn't have to pass him in the hallway. I felt bad telling him no.

"Did someone ask you to go?" It was like she could read my mind.

"Well, David did. But I told him I had to think about it," I told her honestly, refusing to make eye contact. Her face was frozen.

"Claire Elizabeth Walker.. You mean to tell me that DAVID WILES asked you to the prom, and you never told me!?" She was shocked, and her voice sounded betrayed.

"I didn't know if I would feel up to going," I told her truthfully. "And I never gave him an answer, so, it's not like I can just tell him now - a week away - sure, David, I'll be your date. Hopefully your tux matches my dress that I don't have!" I said sarcastically. Jaquelyn would understand that events like prom require advanced preparation.

"Well when did he ask you?" She wanted to know all of the details; every single one of them.

"About a week ago," I told her. "He asked me at my locker. Nothing cutesy or anything like that". Jon had found a way to break into Jacquelyn's locker and put a large poster that said 'Prom? Please!' with a dozen roses. She found it while switching out her books in between classes. *That* was cutesy.

"I think you should go with him, Claire," Jacquelyn said matter-of-factly. "I think you've been down, and dances are fun and up-lifting. It would be good for you." She tried to sound convincing.

Surprisingly, at that exact moment, I wasn't totally against the idea. Maybe she was right. It might get my mind off of Benjamin, if only for one night. As much as I loved him and didn't ever want to forget about him completely, I knew that my mental health was suffering.

"Do you think it's too late to say yes?" I wondered aloud. I saw Jacquelyn's face get really excited. She jumped up and down.

"No! I bet he'd love that!" She shrieked, nearly dropping the dress that was in her hands. "Now, let's find you a dress!"

We spent the next half hour browsing through dresses. Jacquelyn picked up the navy velvet dress, but I immediately told her that it wasn't for me. The truth was, I wouldn't be able to forget about Benjamin if I was wearing a dress that reminded me of him all night. And as much as I loved Benjamin, I did think my brain needed just a small break; a little peace and quiet.

I found a purple dress on the clearance rack for 50% off. It was from last year's collection, but it was in my size. I didn't even try it on first before buying it. I literally brought it up to the counter and reached for the debit card my dad lent me. Jacquelyn tried on a few different dresses, and eventually picked a light pink tight-fitted dress. It looked beautiful on her, like everything always did.

CHAPTER 4: When I Almost Forgot

It was the evening of the Senior Prom at Trenton High and you could feel the excitement in the air. I decided to tell David that I'd go with him, and I wish I could have taken a picture of how shocked he looked. I think he thought I was going to blow him off. But, I didn't, and he ended up being able to find a purple bow tie that almost matched my dress perfectly.

Jacquelyn, Jon, David, and I took a limousine to the prom with a few other friends from school. The kids were extra rowdy, and although it was noisy, I had to admit, I was starting to enjoy myself.

The prom was held at a fancy restaurant and banquet hall called *Mandel's*, only a block away from the high school. Once we arrived, our senior class advisers were there with microphones to introduce each couple as they entered. Jacquelyn and Jon were introduced first, and then David and I.

"Next we have senior David Wiles escorting senior Claire Walker," one of the advisers spoke into the mic. People clapped. I felt ridiculous with all that attention on me, even if it was only for a few minutes. I couldn't wait to get into the restaurant and sit down for dinner.

Dinner was actually delicious. We sat at a large, round table with beautiful floral arrangements in the center. The room looked more like a wedding than a prom. Leave it to Trenton's seniors to do that - many families in our town had a lot of money, including Jacquelyn's.

For my meal, I had an amazing pasta primavera dish, and David had filet mignon. We both drank Coke. It didn't feel awkward sitting next to David, or even eating next to him. It hadn't felt weird in the limo, either. He was actually really easy to talk to. I remembered last year when the two of us sat next to each other at lunch every day. Our conversations seemed to flow seamlessly. A little part of me started to remember the feelings that I used to have for him.

"Do you want to dance?" He asked, as we both finished our meals. I looked over to the dance floor. There were a few couples dancing, but not many.

"Oh, I don't know..." I started to think of an excuse. Dancing wasn't really my thing. I always felt slightly ridiculous dancing.

"Come on, Claire," He insisted. "It'll be fun." He smiled and winked at me. David was charming.

"Fine," I said, throwing my napkin from my lap to the table as I stood. "Let's go dance."

Jacquelyn saw us standing and grabbed Jon's arm. "Come on, let's go!" She said hurriedly. She pulled him onto the dance floor behind us.

It was a fast song and it actually felt good to dance. I let the music take over my body and swayed around with Jacquelyn, David, and Jon. I felt carefree, maybe even happy. I didn't care who was watching. I liked that feeling and longed for it to stay. It had been such a long time since I'd felt it.

The song ended and another fast song came on. We continued to dance - the four of us forming a circle. I looked around at all the happy faces. For a brief moment, I wondered if I would be okay.

And then a slow song came on. Jacquelyn and Jon immediately

grabbed one another. David held his hand out to me. I looked down at his hand, not taking it right away. It was so nice of him to invite me to the prom; to get me out of the house. I would just be sitting home right now, pining away for Benjamin, if it wasn't for David.

"Sure," I said, as I grabbed his hand and placed it on my waist. I put my arms around his neck and he smiled at me. I smiled back. This wasn't so bad. We swayed to the music.

"Are you having fun?" David asked as we danced. His dark eyes looked even darker in the dim-lit room.

"Yes," I told him honestly. I couldn't believe it, but it was true. I was actually enjoying myself.

"Good," He said, smiling. He did have a nice smile. I smiled back. *Do you know who else has a nice smile?* My brain teased. *Yes, I know.* I tried to shut it up. I was finally having fun, not crying or pouting or staring blankly out a window. How dare my brain betray me like that!

But it was no use. As soon as the thought of Benjamin's smile came into my mind, it was all I could think about. I pictured dancing there with Benjamin, not David. I pictured Benjamin's arms around my waist, and me staring into Benjamin's eyes. I remembered Benjamin's scent and the way he would always cradle my face when he kissed me...

So when David leaned in to kiss me, I kissed him back. I simply envisioned Benjamin.

For a moment, it was glorious. But soon, reality hit me, and I realized what I was doing. I backed away quickly.

"I'm so sorry!" I said, pushing David away. I put my hands on my lips. I couldn't believe I just did that. I needed some fresh air. I ran outside of the restaurant as quickly as I could.

When I got outside, there were couples making out, some kids puking in the bushes, and others standing around waiting for their ride to pick them up. They looked at me. *I need to get out of here.* It felt like I couldn't breathe; like my chest was closing in on itself. I briefly wondered if I was having an anxiety attack.

I searched around quickly, and decided to head back to the school. It was only a block away. I could call my father to come pick me up. *Crap*, I remembered. *My phone is in my purse on my seat, still inside the restaurant.* Oh well.

But I couldn't wait there. I didn't want to. I had to get away. I kicked off my heels, carrying them in my right hand, and started running towards the school.

"Claire!" I heard David and Jacquelyn yelling behind me. They were trying to follow me. I just kept running.

When I got to the school, it was pitch black, with no one in sight. *Great*, I thought, *now what?* I looked around. It was super dark, except for the moon. The moon was bright, vibrant, and full. A full moon? I didn't realize tonight was going to be a full moon. I slowly walked towards it, taking in its beauty and remembering the power it had over Benjamin. That's when I saw it.

It was huge. And black. Just waiting, docked at the edge of the pier. A ship. Not just any ship. A pirate ship. A pirate ship on a full moon. I'd had dreams of finding a pirate ship waiting underneath the light of the full moon for weeks.

I knew exactly what I had to do.

I took off running down the pier as quickly as I could. I had no idea when the ship had docked, but I didn't want to miss it leaving. I had to move quickly. Behind me, I heard Jacquelyn, Jon, and David calling my name and telling me to slow down.

"Claire! Don't! It's dangerous!" Jacquelyn screamed. But she continued running after me.

"I'm sorry, Claire," David shouted. He didn't stop running, either.

I was about fifty feet from the edge of the pier now, and I could see the ship close up. I stopped. A green flag whipped in the wind. *Oh no. That's* not *The Serpent's Skull.* I remembered that ship, though. I had seen it before - when I was taken off Benjamin's ship and thrown onto it. It was Captain Brooks' ship. Brooks was not a nice man. I had to get out of there, and fast!

I turned to run back towards the school, but stopped when I saw Jacquelyn, Jon, and David being dragged towards the ship by what I could only assume were pirates.

"Claire! Run!" Jacquelyn screamed, as she struggled in her captor's arms. The pirates snickered, cursing as they dragged my friends along. I turned back to the ship. There was nowhere for me to run. I was trapped.

I thought about getting into the water. I was a great swimmer. I could try to hide there until they were gone. Unfortunately, one of the captors saw me and grabbed me before I could put my plan into action.

And that's the night I was kidnapped by pirates for the second time.

CHAPTER 5: Not Again

I looked over at Jacquelyn. I'm so sorry, I tried to tell her telepathically. Our captors had us gagged with our arms tied to the railings of the deck. I was hoping she would see the remorse in my eyes.

It was still night. David and Jon looked completely terrified. I remembered the first time that I was kidnapped on the pier, and I felt so sorry for them. Of course, it was worse this time because it actually was my fault. I was so stupid! I knew better than to be on the pier at night.

"How many are there?" I heard a loud voice ask, one full of authority. I knew immediately that it belonged to Captain Matthew Brooks.

"Four, Captain. Two lassies," a dirty pirate answered. "Must be our lucky night!" They all chuckled.

Captain Brooks came over to get a closer look. He started with the boys. He stared at each of them for only a few seconds. Then, he moved on to Jacquelyn. He got close enough to touch her hair. I started screaming for him to get his hands off of her, even though there was a gag over my mouth. He quickly turned his eyes towards me.

"Well, well, well…" he said, as he walked over, closer. "You look awfully familiar, lass" he said. "Weren't you Stantun's little pet?" How dare he.

I simply glared at him. After all, I wasn't able to speak. After a moment, he pulled the gag down so that it hung on my neck.

"I'm nobody's pet!" I said, disgusted.

"He very nearly killed himself trying to rescue you," Brooks recalled. "You must be important to him."

My mind flashed back to the time that I was taken by Brooks' men from The Serpent's Skull to the very ship I was on now. Benjamin had followed me, even though he was cursed and by leaving his own ship, he experienced unbearable pain. It very nearly killed him. But he followed me, nonetheless, making sure that I was safely returned to The Serpent's Skull.

I thought about how much Brooks hated Benjamin. Would he kill me just to spite him? After all, Benjamin's father had killed Brooks' love just to spite him. Leave it to the universe to bring it all back around, full circle.

I decided that I wouldn't mention Benjamin; I didn't want to give Brooks any ideas. Besides, I had an idea of my own.

"I'm important to you," I informed him. Captain Brooks was my great-great-great grandfather, trapped in some weird, hard to process, time loop. Though, he didn't know it. He snickered.

"I very highly doubt that," He said. The other pirates chuckled.

I'm just going to go for it, I thought. "I'm your granddaughter," I said. He didn't even flinch.

"Who told you to say that?" He asked, intrigued. He stood there, looking at me cautiously from top to bottom. His eyes squinted.

"Nobody told me to say it. It's true. I'm the granddaughter of Amara, Arabelle's daughter," I said. His eyes froze.

Captain Brooks reached for his sword and pulled it out.

"How dare you," He started. Jacquelyn was screaming, only it was muffled because she was gagged.

"It's true!" I exclaimed, shocked that he would think I was lying." How would I even know who Amara and Arabelle are?

"Where did you hear those names from? Stantun?" He accused. He was furious now.

"Actually, it was a witch." I paused to look over at my friends. Jacquelyn was visibly upset. The boys looked like they were about to throw up any minute.

"A witch showed me the past.. *My* past. My great-great grand-mother was Amara, your daughter," I assured him.

"Witches are evil," He said simply before turning his head to spit on the deck.

"Then why did you fall in love with one?" I asked. He simply stared at me without blinking. "Arabelle was one of the most tal-ented witches there ever was." I remembered Genevieve telling me that.

Brooks looked down. I could sense sadness radiating from him. It made me feel bad, but what was I supposed to do? Just let this monster kill me?!

"They died," He simply said, not looking up. "I have no children, and no grandchildren." His voice was full of sorrow.

"Arabelle died. Amara lived," I corrected him. "She was raised by someone else."

"How would you know that?" He asked, doubtful. I could tell that he didn't believe me.

"I told you... a witch showed me. She showed me Arabelle on a deck with Captain Stantun…" I trailed off. Brooks' face showed his fury. I quickly skipped over all the bad parts. "Arabelle sent Amara to be with someone who would keep her safe. Someone who didn't mess around with pirates. She lived a happy life and had children, and her children had children. My mother was one of her descendents, and so am I." He looked me over.

"We all have the same light hair and green eyes," I reminded him, trying to persuade him further. He got close enough to touch my hair again. He held it in his hands, and looked my face over curiously.

"Witches are evil," he simply said again, after about a minute. "You should stay away from them." And then he walked away. The four of us were left on that top deck for the night, tied to its railings.

CHAPTER 6: Old Friends

When I woke in the morning, the sun was hot on my skin. My neck ached fiercely from having to sleep sitting up. I looked over at my friends. How could I ever make this up to them?

I heard men walking around, drinking spirits, moving supplies, and positioning the sails. Typical pirate stuff.

"Bring me the crates from below, Joe," Captain Brooks ordered. I looked over and saw Joe, the not-so-friendly pirate from Benjamin's ship. I gasped. He heard me and smiled a wicked smile. I wondered how he'd gotten onto Brooks' ship. Then I started to worry about Benjamin.. Was he okay? Was his ship okay?

"Ay ay, Captain," Joe replied. He went below deck to retrieve the crates.

"Joe?" I asked, when he returned. He simply looked at me, not coming any closer. "What are you doing here? Is Benjamin okay?" I asked, the fear present in my voice.

His face was expressionless. He glanced around to see if anyone was watching. Then, slowly, carefully, he approached me. He stopped about five feet away.

"I left The Serpent's Skull on the last moon," He simply said, with no emotion whatsoever.

"Why?" I inquired. Joe was Benjamin's right-hand man.

"I was sick of the curse." He looked me up and down and scoffed.

Of course, he knew I could break the curse on the ship. To him, I was the most vile creature upon the face of the earth.

"I don't like not being in control, lass," He further explained. "On The Skull, I had no say. What Stantun ordered, I had to do. Plus, I was second-in-command. It started eatin' away at me.. The notion that if Benjamin died for some reason, it'd be me stuck as the Captain of that dreadful ship. Then I'd be the one cursed." I could tell he'd put a lot of thought into it.

"So when we docked, I left to get supplies and never came back. I hoped The Golden Green would be docked a few miles East, and as luck had it, it was. I ran to join them." He put his head down. It was almost as if he felt a little bit ashamed of his decision to abandon Benjamin and his men.

"What about Benjamin?" I asked. He was all I really cared about.

"Fine, as far as I know," Joe replied. "He's lost lots of crew this way over the years. In fact, there was a group of us who came to this ship that night." I looked around. I didn't recognize any of them.

I put my head down. Tears started rolling down my face. "I wonder if I'll ever see him again," I confided quietly.

Joe didn't move. He simply watched me. "I wouldn't worry too much about it," was all he said before he turned to walk away.

CHAPTER 7: Let's Make A Trade

It had been a whole 24-hours since we'd been tied up to the railings on that ship. No food, no water, and the hot sun beating down on us all day. The others had fallen asleep. Well, passed out, is more like it. I sat there, my eyes tired but my head desperately trying to hatch a plan to escape. There wasn't much we could do on our own, being tied up and all. I knew I'd have to have help.

Interrupting my thoughts, I heard the thud of loud steel boots. I knew who they belonged to.

"Evening, lass," Brooks said, gently tipping his hat.

I simply stared at him with disgust. Was this the way he treated his own family?

"Joe had a talk with me this afternoon," He started. "He said Stantun would do literally anything to have you returned to him unharmed and in one piece. Do you know what that means?" He waited. I continued to sit still, not answering him.

"It means that I have a treasure - something he wants. And in order to get it, he'll have to give me what I want," He sounded evil.

"What do you want?" I simply asked, in a disgusted voice. Though, I was terrified of the answer.

"I want his ship," He said, matter-of-factly.

"But he's the Captain of that ship," I reminded him. If Brooks wanted to take The Serpent's Skull as his own, what would become of Benjamin?

"That's because it's his ship, lassie. If it were my own ship, I'd be the Captain. I'd add the ship to my fleet, and we'd be unstoppable." He sounded a little crazed, but also excited.

I thought for a moment. *Brooks must not realize that The Serpent's Skull is cursed. He must think it's Benjamin who's cursed. But really, whoever is the Captain of the ship is the one with the curse upon him.*

I thought about Arabelle, and how much she adored Captain Brooks. She would have *never* placed a curse on him - not on the father of her own child. Just like she wouldn't have purposely made it so that *I* was the only one who could break the curse - her very own descendent. Maybe it was good advice not to mess around with all this witch business. I could see how things ended up differently than Arabelle originally planned. Maybe it was best to stay as far away from it all as possible, as my grandfather Brooks had insisted.

"You can't do that," I said, sounding wise beyond my years.

"Oh yeah?" He chucked. "I think I can." He winked. He reached for the flask in his pocket and took a big swig. He wiped his mouth with the sleeve of his coat afterwards.

"Then you'll be cursed," I simply said. He looked at me curiously.

"Stantun's cursed, and for good reason. Him and his father were the lowest scum of the Earth," He spat the words. He took another drink.

"That's not true," I said. I waited for him to inquire more. He simply stood and waited for me to continue.

"I'd love to tell you all about it," I started. "But I'm a little bit hungry, and my wrists hurt," I said, looking down. I was hoping he'd set me free from these ties. This was the first part of my plan.

He looked at me skeptically, and then came over and cut the rope with his sword. I pulled my wrists toward me. They were red, and the skin was starting to break. I rubbed them.

"Could you please untie my friends?" I asked. He smirked, but then thought for a moment.

"If you tell me everything you know about Stantun's curse, I'll untie your friends." He said.

"And ungag them," I added. My plan was working perfectly.

He nodded. I nodded. He freed them and they woke, startled.

"What's going on?" Jacquelyn asked, exhausted.

"Captain Brooks was just helping us to be a little more comfortable," I told her, all the while watching Brooks. I didn't trust him, not even a little.

My friends seemed relieved.

"Joe!" Brooks called. "Come bring these three below. Clean them up and get them some dinner," He ordered.

Joe came and took my friends. It was just Brooks and me.

"Now," Brooks started. "Tell me what you know."

I thought about how much I should tell him. I'd already told him that I was his granddaughter, and he didn't believe me. Would he believe me if I told him it was Arabelle who placed the curse on Stantun's ship? Should I leave that part out? I thought for a moment, but he interrupted me.

"Well…" he pried. He waited impatiently.

I had heard it was best to always tell the truth. I figured I'd try to tell him everything I knew. If he didn't believe me, that was on him.

"I went to visit a witch," I started. I heard him exhale in disbelief. He shook his head. "She showed me the past. In it, Arabelle placed a curse on Benjamin's father's ship - The Serpent's Skull. Whomever was its Captain was stuck on that ship forever. She placed the ship in a time loop - one they couldn't escape unless the curse was broken. It stays in limbo on the sea, and can only dock on a full moon to get supplies," I told him. "So, at first it was Benjamin's father who was cursed. But when he died, Benjamin became the Captain, and so then curse was on him." It made me sad saying it aloud.

Brooks didn't so much as flinch.

"So, if you take over his ship, the curse would be on you. The person who's cursed is whoever is the Captain of that ship," I told him. His eyes moved around, and I could tell he was processing what I was saying.

"Why did," he paused. He seemed to struggle briefly, "Arabelle… Why did she place a curse on him to begin with?" I could feel the pain escaping him. It was strange to think that pirates had feelings. But I knew how much he'd loved her. And she had loved him also.

"It was right before he killed her," I simply said, refusing to make eye contact with him. He didn't blink.

"And you're telling me.. The child escaped? Unharmed? " He asked. He remembered what I'd said last night.

"Yes. Arabelle gave her to someone she knew; someone to raise her and keep her safe. She survived," I said. He came closer to me and tugged on a piece of my long blonde hair.

We talked for what seemed like hours. I kept telling Brooks everything I knew about the curse, except for how it can be broken. I didn't want him to know that part. He nodded carefully and I could tell he was up to something, some type of plan.

When he'd heard enough, he simply said, "I believe you, lass. You're right - you have her hair and her eyes." He smiled briefly as he touched my face with his fingertips, before retreating his hand. "I don't want you to take this the wrong way, but I feel, as your grandfather, that I should be honest with you."

I waited, scared to hear the rest.

"I still have to use you as bait, lassie," he stated matter-of-factly. "Maybe I don't want to be Captain of that ship - I certainly don't want to be cursed. But, there's valuables on that ship that would come in mighty handy. And I like valuables."

He was repulsive. I couldn't believe that I was actually somehow related to this man.

"Benjamin isn't going to fall for your tricks," I shouted. But who was I kidding? Benjamin had literally risked his life to save me a few months ago. I worried that he would be willing to do or give away anything to make sure I was safe.

"Oh lass," Brooks chucked. "I have no tricks up my sleeve. I intend to do this in a very honest manner. I have something he wants," he titled his head in my direction. "And he has quite a few things that I want. It's an even trade, fair and square."

I scoffed. Nothing about pirates was fair, even I knew that. I was almost certain Brooks did have a trick up his sleeve, but I decided to pretend like I believed him. Actually, according to what Brooks was saying, it seemed like he might lead me right to Benjamin. My heart started skipping frantically at the thought.

"Well," I started, "that seems like a fair trade to me." I was just happy to see Benjamin again. I spent the remainder of the evening daydreaming about how wonderful our reunion would be.

CHAPTER 8: Time For A Plan

The next day, Joe woke me in the very early hours.

"Hey, Miss," he whispered. He shook my shoulder.

I mumbled. I had spent all night daydreaming about Benjamin and hadn't really gotten a good night's rest.

"I have an idea," he whispered again.

I waited, blinking, trying to wake up completely.

"The Captain wants to trade you for some things off The Serpent's Skull," Joe said, in a low voice. I already knew this. Brooks had told me all about his plan last night.

"I heard," I simply said. I was so tired.

"I know what he wants," he stated.

I was awake and intrigued. "What is it that he wants?" I asked in a low whisper.

"There's treasure on that ship, lass. Stantun's father had travelled all over the world collecting precious gems, jewels, and gold coins. I know where he keeps it all. When we docked, it's what he used to give the crew to trade for supplies. The problem is, that's all Stantun has to trade with. If he loses the treasure, he loses everything. He has no way to get off the ship and get more. He'll starve to death. I think that's Brooks' plan," he insisted.

I thought about what he was saying. "How much treasure is

there?" I asked. I smirked a little, hearing myself say it. How ridiculous to be talking about treasure, although not too much surprised me anymore.

"There used to be loads and loads. That's how the Skull became the most powerful ship in the sea - they had everything. Over the years, it has definitely dwindled down. But I reckon there's still probably enough to last him another year or two."

I mused. I hadn't realized Benjamin would ever be in danger of starving. The thought made me sad.

"We can't let Brooks trade you for the treasure," Joe said matter-of-factly. "We've got to get you off this ship before the trade takes place."

"Why are you helping me?" I suddenly asked. Trying to figure out the mind games these pirates play was exhausting. I didn't think I could take much more of it.

Joe hung his head. "Stantun was always good to me," he started. "I'm not going to pretend like I'm righteous. I know what I am - a pirate through and through. Stantun's not like me, he's not like any of us. He's... he's a good person."

He was telling me things I'd figured out a long, long time ago.

"I feel bad having to leave him the way I did," he finally admitted. He exhaled. "He was always good to me. He's saved my life so many times I lost track. If I can get you back to him, safely, well, I'd feel a lot better about the way it all worked out."

"But if you help me, Captain Brooks will surely know and you'll be a dead man," I spoke the obvious.

Joe looked down. His eyes got teary. I think I went into a little bit of shock, seeing him like that.

"This might sound crazy to you, lassie, but I think I've had enough of being a pirate. I think I'm ready to make a life for myself on the shore," he spoke slowly, with his head down the whole time.

This was not the first time I'd heard a pirate say that they were tired of being a pirate. Benjamin had admitted this to me, of course. But for some reason, it completely surprised me coming from Joe. He seemed like the perfect fit to be a pirate.

"I saw the way Benjamin looked at you," Joe continued. "I'd like to have that, with someone, someday. Someone who chooses to be with me of her own free will," he said. I thought about all the unfortunate women who never got that choice and scowled.

Was I being duped? This was the pirate who hit me the first night that I was taken captive on The Serpent's Skull. He had been playing darts using Jacquelyn as a bullseye. Was I supposed to believe that he now magically changed into a caring, decent human being? I don't know… I couldn't tell. He seemed to be sincere, but my mind told me not to accept everything at face value just yet.

"It's normal to want to settle down," I assured him. I didn't know how sincere he actually was, or how much of what he was saying was for show. But I knew that if I stuck to my plan, I would be reunited with Benjamin. I had to keep my eyes on the prize.

"Ay," he simply said, smiling. "So will you let me help you?"

I smiled. "Of course," I said. I put my hand out to shake his, even though the thought of touching him would have previously made me vomit. I needed to see Benjamin.

"Alright then, here's the plan…" Joe started, reaching his hand to meet mine. He told me that Benjamin's ship usually docks at a certain place this month on the full month. He was 90% sure they'd dock there on the next moon, and he thought he could convince Brooks to also dock a few miles away. He said he'd help us escape, come with us, and he'd lead the way to Benjamin's ship. I thought about all the ways we could get caught; about all the things that could go wrong. But in the end, I decided that it would be worth it even just to try. Anything would be worth it to be with Benjamin.

CHAPTER 9: Escape
In The Night

It felt like the days dragged on and on with no end in sight. As far as I knew, Joe's plan was set to work on the next full moon. The only thing was, it was weeks away, and trying to pass the time on that ship with those vile pirates was not easy.

Captain Brooks was not mean to me or my friends, but he wasn't very nice either. He was indifferent. He let us eat one meal a day and allowed us to sleep downstairs, away from the blazing sun. David and Jon were still in total disbelief about what happened, but Jacquelyn was acting like her normal self. The boys were very quiet, always looking around cautiously. Joe stayed away from all of us, not wanting anyone to know he was planning to help us escape.

Finally, the weeks passed and it was time for us to make our escape. Joe told me the night before. We spent the following day preparing. I looked around for things we might need, hiding them in my dress. I found a rope, a pocket knife, an apple (in case I got hungry), and I filled a canteen with rain water the crew had collected.

Because we were docked, Brooks assigned a crew member to guard the four of us, probably to make sure we didn't escape. He hadn't assigned anyone to guard us before, but I guess there was no place to really escape up until then, unless we wanted to jump overboard and become fish food, which we definitely did not want.

An hour went by. Then another. And then another. I was starting to get worried that Joe had lied to me. Had he gotten my hopes up for nothing? I looked around. I would attempt to escape by myself, if I had to. I couldn't bear the thought of another month on that awful ship.

"How's it going, lad?" Joe asked the guard, as he walked towards the group of us.

"Good. Just guarding these here prisoners," the man replied. He had his hand on the top of his sword.

"I see," Joe said, walking closer. The man just looked at him.

"That one's mighty pretty," Joe said, nodding over to Jacquelyn. The man fell for the trap, and turned his eyes to look. That's when Joe came up behind him, covering his face with some sort of cloth. The man struggled for a second and then fell to the ground.

Joe quickly slid the man's body to the edge of the ship. He covered him with large brown sacks - some full and some empty.

"Hurry now," he said to the four of us. I hadn't told the boys about the plan. They seemed too nervous, and I didn't know how much I could trust them. I couldn't risk anything about tonight getting messed up. Of course, I told Jacquelyn everything. She was the most trustworthy person I knew. And the thought of escaping gave her hope, something I was happy to offer. After all, I still felt horribly guilty for being the reason that we were all in this mess in the first place.

"Let's go!" Joe whispered, frantically. There was a rope tied to the dock leading to the waters below.

"You're not serious?!" Jacquelyn argued. Her eyes were full of fear.

"Come on, Jacquelyn. It's our only hope!" I assured her. I went first, to show them that it was sturdy, even though I didn't know whether or not that was even true.

One by one, we carefully climbed down the rope and gently eased our way into the water below. The water was freezing, which was unusual for the time of the year.

We heard Brooks' crew loading and unloading crates onto the pier. Joe motioned for us to be silent. I knew if any of them found us trying to escape, that would be the end. I would never see Benjamin again. That was all the motivation I needed to keep low and quiet.

Someone started walking in our direction with a light. Joe motioned for us to hide under the dock. I looked over and saw Jacquelyn shivering. I squeezed her hand. She looked at me, faking a smile.

"How many bottles did they have?" it was Brooks' voice, coming from directly above us on the dock.

"Only a dozen, Captain," someone else responded. Their voices drifted off as they walked further away, getting closer to boarding back onto the ship.

I looked at Joe. He shook his head. We needed to wait a little bit longer.

Finally, Joe motioned for us to quietly follow him. He waded onto the other side of the deck; opposite of the ship. We quickly followed and I was relieved to no longer be able to see the dreaded boat that I'd been held captive on for the past few weeks.

Just when my breathing finally felt normal again, lights started shining frantically all around us onto the water. Next, came the shouting.

"I don't know, Captain. I don't see any of them over here!" someone shouted.

"Southside is clear!" someone else yelled.

I looked at Joe nervously. They'd realized we were missing. I didn't know how likely it was that we'd actually escape, but I always had hope. That hope seemed to disappear into thin air now.

I could tell Joe was calculating. I knew if there was any chance of us surviving this, we'd have to trust him. He knew pirates. He *was* a pirate. And he'd be in just as much trouble as us, if not more, if we got caught.

After a few seconds which seemed to last for an eternity, Joe signaled for us to follow him. We slowly made our way closer to the shore, one foot at a time. At one point, lights were shining in our direction, and Joe held his breath and completely submerged himself under the water. The four of us followed his lead.

Under the water, I opened my eyes carefully in search of Joe. He was swimming towards me, and grabbed my hand to pull me with him. The other three followed us. He seemed to be bringing us out to deeper water now. I longed to be back onto the shore, but I knew I had to trust him. I continued to swim after him.

After a minute or so, he went to the surface for air. Soon, we were all gasping to fill our lungs with fresh oxygen. Trying to do so quietly was quite the challenge. I looked around to see where we had swam to. We were definitely farther out, far away from the ship and the search lights.

"Are you strong swimmers?" Joe asked us. We all nodded. I was suddenly happy for all the lessons my father had paid for to keep me busy after my mother died.

"We're going to have to swim a ways," he said. And then he turned and the rest of us followed.

We swam for about twenty minutes or so, and my body was exhausted. But whenever I felt like giving up, I simply thought about Benjamin. And then I knew that I had to try harder.

Eventually, Joe brought us to a rocky area of shore. We continued to see The Golden Green behind us in the distance. It still was docked, likely searching for its escapees.

When we finally managed to make it onto the shore, we were exhausted. The four of us tumbled to the ground. Joe did not.

"Come on," he insisted. "There's no time to waste. They'll find us." He glanced up at the moon. "Plus, we're running out of time."

We slowly picked ourselves back up and followed him. He started jogging, and as painful as it was, so did we. I could hear Jacquelyn whimpering, but I didn't even have the energy to encourage her. I just kept up the pace and kept my mind on the prize.

We jogged for about three miles. Three long, awful, exhausting, freezing-cold-because-we-were-soaking-wet miles. But miraculously enough, when I saw the black silhouette that I remembered vividly from my nightly dreams in the near distance, all the pain vanished.

I could *feel* him. Even though I couldn't see him, I could *feel* him. He was close.

I suddenly felt like I had so much energy. I started sprinting towards The Serpent's Skull.

Joe stopped abruptly in front of me. I very nearly ran him over.

"Come on, what are you doing?" I asked, confused.

"This is it for me, Miss. I brought you to Stantun's ship, like I said I would. You'll have to go the rest of the way on your own," he smiled and then he was gone. I felt bad. I was so busy trying to comprehend what was happening while at the same time trying hard not to get hypothermia, that I didn't even get a chance to thank him.

"Where are we going?" Jon asked. I hadn't realized that he and David still didn't know what the plan was.

"We're going to be rescued," I told them. It wasn't a total lie. Yes, they would still be on a pirate ship. Yes, they wouldn't be home. Yes, it was all against their will. But, I knew Benjamin would make sure my friends weren't harmed. He would know how to get them home, and he would bring them there safely.

"Follow me," I said. I knew the entire blueprint of The Serpent's Skull. Benjamin had always let me roam the ship freely, and I'd explored it from top to bottom. There were some parts that scared me, so I stayed away from them. But I knew where they were and what they were. I knew how to get us onto that ship.

The others followed me as we hid behind bushes and made our way closer. There was a small hatch on the far side of the ship, opposite from where the crew was loading and unloading supplies. I figured it was our safest chance to get onboard without getting caught. Who was I kidding? They'd never even think to look for people actually *trying* to make it onto a dangerous pirate ship. Maybe my father was right to demand I attend weekly counseling sessions.

When nobody was looking, we lowered ourselves into the water and swam to the other side of the ship. We pulled ourselves up using the rope attached to the anchor. We climbed all the way to the top deck and hauled ourselves over the railing and onboard.

I stood up. I was soaking wet, and exhausted. I searched around, hoping to find him.

He was standing about twenty feet away from us. I smiled widely as our eyes met.

CHAPTER 10: Reunited
And It Feels So Good

"Claire," the most beautiful voice in the universe breathed. He squinted his eyes and turned his head slightly.

"Benjamin!" I ran to him. He was too shocked to move, and it took him a minute to register that I was really there, in the flesh. He smelled my hair and breathed me in, and then he wrapped his arms tightly around my waist and nuzzled his face in my neck.

"What are you doing here?" he asked, perplexed. He looked around at us. We were wearing prom dresses and tuxedos that were soaked, dirty, bloodstained, and torn. I was sure we looked like characters who'd just escaped a very scary film.

"I love you," I simply said. He grabbed my face as he held back tears. He smiled sweetly and then kissed me with the passion that only a man who's been forced to be apart from the woman he loves could. I heard David clear his throat.

"I love you," he said back. "More than anything." He was rubbing my face. He placed his thumb on my lower lip and bent to touch his forehead to mine. "You have no idea how much I've missed you," he choked out the words. I had never seen Benjamin so emotional before.

"I can imagine it's nearly as much as I've missed you," I replied. I grabbed his face and kissed him again.

"How did you get here?" he asked, as he ran his hands playfully through my hair. He stopped to smell my hair in his hands every so often.

"I was on the pier again at night.." I started. He was going to think I was an absolute fool. Had I learned nothing from my last experience? "It was a full moon. I saw a ship... And I thought it was yours! It was big and black.. And I just so desperately wanted to see you again. I ran towards it. My friends followed me," I said, nodding back to the three behind me. "Once I was close enough to realize that it wasn't The Serpent's Skull, it was too late. I was being kidnapped.. Again! It was The Golden Green.. Brooks' ship!" I didn't dare look him in the eye. But I heard his breath turn heavy. "He only cared about keeping me alive so that he could use me as ransom with you." I paused to check Benjamin's expression. He was intrigued to know more.

"You are still the most reckless human I've ever met," Benjamin said matter-of-factly.

"Joe was there," I started again. Benjamin scowled. I knew Joe had left him to go work for Stantun, but I wanted him to know that he had actually helped us. And that he felt bad about leaving Benjamin.

"He helped me. He knew where you'd be docking during the next full moon and he convinced Stantun to dock as well, a few miles over. He told him that you would give *anything*, anything at all to have me alive and in one piece. Stantun agreed to dock, and Joe helped us to escape. We ran three miles to find you!" I exclaimed. I'd secretly hoped he would appreciate that because I absolutely *hated* to run.

"Claire," Benjamin whispered, placing his hands back on my face and looking me over curiously. "Did anybody hurt you?" he asked. I could tell that he would not take it lightly if they had.

"No, I mean… I have some bruises but nothing serious." I admitted. My wrists still hurt quite a bit from being tied so tightly to the railings with rope.

"And none of the men *touched* you?" he pried. I knew what he meant.

"No," I assured him. "I'm totally fine." I looked up to see him smiling and relieved. His eyes were closed and he looked happy.

"We have to get my friends back," I said quickly, before I lost myself in Benjamin's eyes and forgot all about them. Benjamin peered over at them.

"Hello, Jacquelyn," he said politely with a smile. She smiled back.

"And that's Jon.. and there's David," I introduced the boys by pointing to them. They both smiled and nodded cautiously. Benjamin smiled back, but not before taking a long hard look at David.

CHAPTER 11: Confessions
Of A Prom Goer

Benjamin brought us dry clothes and showed everyone their sleeping quarters. Jacquelyn, Jon, and David got to sleep in the crew's area, which was a nice change of scenery for Jacquelyn. Last time, she was stuck with the prisoners. The crew's area was a large room with lots of bunks. It smelled of mold and rum, of course, but it was spacious.

I said goodnight to my friends and walked with Benjamin back to his sleeping quarters. He held the door open for me.

"After you, my lady," he said sweetly. I simply smiled and kissed him as I walked by.

"Is that the David you intended to marry?" he asked playfully, as he put away his coat and hat.

I laughed. He had a memory like an elephant.

"I told you that I made that whole thing up!" I headed towards the bed. I desperately longed for a good night's sleep.

"How did he get here with you?" he asked. His voice was turning softer. I detected a hint of jealousy.

"Well," I began, "We went to the prom together." I checked Benjamin's face for understanding. He looked confused. "It's a dance, where people dress up." I whirled around in the dry shirt Benjamin had brought me, pretending to dance.

"With music?" he asked. I forgot that there probably weren't proms back in Benjamin's time. At least he was able to make the connection to music.

"Yes," I agreed. "There's music, and people dress up and they go and dance to the music."

"So you danced with David?" he concluded. *Yup*, I thought, *he is definitely jealous.*

I put my head down, a little ashamed. Here I was declaring my unconditional love for this man with my prom date waiting in a nearby room. I couldn't lie to Benjamin.

"Yes, I danced with him," I said, head down. "He was my date."

"Your date?" he asked, perplexed.

"Yes, he asked me to go to the prom with him. And I said yes." There. That was the whole truth.

"Interesting," was all Benjamin could say. He continued to stare at my face, his eyes squinting every once in a while. I knew it was ridiculous for him to be jealous of David, but it was my fault for making up that stupid engagement story in the first place.

"Benjamin," I started. I grabbed a hold of his hands and waited until he was staring me straight in the eye. "When you left me, it felt like my whole world was shattered. I could barely breathe." I shuddered as I remembered back to those days. There was nothing but darkness there. "I didn't want to even go to the prom, but David asked me to. And Jacquelyn was going with Jon. She thought it would be good for me to get out of the house, maybe try to have a little fun. So I agreed to go with him. But I assure you, I have no feelings for David whatsoever. I love you and only you," I leaned in to kiss him.

He didn't kiss me back. His face was frozen.

"It doesn't matter," I said, "Because the three of them are returning home and then it will just be you and me. Forever."

Benjamin smiled at that idea. But he didn't agree with me, something I took note of.

* **

That first night back with Benjamin was glorious. We kissed, and cuddled, and laughed the whole night. I don't think either one of us slept, as tired as I was. We just kept staring at each other; making sure the other one was real. I admit, I was afraid to fall asleep for fear of waking up and our reunion being nothing but a dream.

CHAPTER 12: Oh Grey Mush, How I Haven't Missed You

The next day, Benjamin completed his morning routine and then we all sat down together for a meal.

"What is this stuff, anyways?" Jon asked, pushing the grey mush around with his fork.

"You get used to it," Jacquelyn insisted. She would know.

"I don't know about that…" he replied.

"Trust me," David said, "If I knew kissing Claire would get me kidnapped and stuck on two pirate ships and that this is what the food was gonna be like, I would have never kissed her!" He laughed.

Benjamin's face turned bright red.

"You *kissed* Claire?" he asked, stern and accusingly. He wrapped his fingers tightly around his utensils.

"Yeah, man. She was my prom date and it was a slow song…" David tried to explain. He could tell Benjamin felt uneasy.

"I pushed him away and ran off," I explained, touching Benjamin's arm lightly. I hoped David would just stop talking. I had a feeling he would just make things worse.

"You never told me you kissed him," Benjamin whispered to me in a sad, accusing voice.

"I forgot all about it, to be honest. And once I realized we were kissing, I freaked out and ran away. That's why I ran out of the dance and to the pier." I explained.

"And why we followed her," Jacquelyn added glumly. She sighed.

Benjamin forced a smile and then nodded. But I didn't like the way he looked back at David.

"We should be home soon, right?" Jon chimed in. I was grateful to him for changing the subject. You could have cut the tension in that room with a knife.

"The next full moon is a whole month from now. That's when we'll dock and you'll be home." Benjamin informed him.

"Can't come soon enough!" David said, eyes down at his plate.

CHAPTER 13: Waiting

The next few weeks were amazing. Well, to me, anyways. I had a feeling the days dragged on and on for the other three and that they couldn't wait for the full moon to be able to get off of The Serpent's Skull.

I spent every second with Benjamin. Being back with him was even better than I'd imagined in all my daydreams and fantasies. He was perfect; *we* were perfect. We were absolutely positively perfect together. We belonged together, and there was no one or nothing that was going to change my mind about that.

I loved Benjamin fiercely. And he loved me, I could feel it when we were together. Benjamin still did not seem eager to take our physical relationship to the next level, unlike me. I was ready and willing and just waiting for him to broach the subject. A few times, while we laid in bed kissing, I moved my hands to unbutton his shirt. I wanted him to know that I wanted him in every way possible. But he just chuckled and slowly pulled my hands away and held them in his own. I never found it odd, though. I knew Benjamin was a gentleman and expected him to behave like one.

Jacquelyn, David, and Jon seemed a little more relaxed than the first night we arrived. I could tell they sensed that they were safe; as I told them they would be. Benjamin simply wouldn't harm a fly. He was such a good man. The more I thought about it, the more angry I got with this stupid curse nonsense. I still couldn't believe my own ancestor would put a curse on the kindest, gentlest, most amazing man in the entire universe.

The days were long and the sun was hot, but I never complained. I was just so happy to finally have Benjamin back in my life. I knew I needed to keep him there, with me. I would do anything.

I approached the subject of *forever* with Benjamin only once. His response scared me, and I didn't dare bring it up again. I was afraid of what he might say.

"You're going to have to teach me how to help out around here, you know?" I teased, as I watched him complete his usual morning tasks. "I don't want to spend all my time walking around and just waiting until you're done. If you let me help, it would take you half as much time," I nudged him softly.

He smirked. "This is no work for a lady, Claire," he said, carrying big crates up and down the stairs.

"Oh yeah? Says who?" I teased some more. "I'm super strong!" I made a muscle with my left arm. I looked down to see it. It was pathetic.

Benjamin laughed. "I know you're strong, my love. But this work was made for a man. Women are caregivers," he said, matter-of-factly.

"So, like, taking care of men?" I asked, knowing that he was from a different time but still a little surprised that he didn't recognize the misogyny of his statement.

"And children," he added, stopping to examine my expression. "I'm sorry, did I say something to upset you?" he asked, genuinely curious.

I blushed and put my head down. I couldn't fault Benjamin for being from a different time - a time when women really did provide the care to children and men really were responsible for the hard labor.

"No, not at all," I lied. I took a deep breath. "I guess, I'm just wondering what life is going to look like for us, out here on this ship, after the others go home," I said.

When he was silent for a few seconds, I carefully looked up at him. His eyes were soft, but pained. Finally, he spoke.

"Are you sure you'd want to choose this life, Claire? You have a life, a family, and a future back home. You'll miss all that," he simply said.

I could feel the rage start to build inside of me. "I absolutely choose you! I choose you over everything!" I shouted, astonished that I even had to say it. Was he insane?! Did he not realize everything I'd been through to reunite with him?!

"You are the most determined person I've ever met," he said sweetly. "I understand your feelings for me. But you're stuck in the present moment. You should think about your future," he suggested.

"That's funny…" I started, "Back home, every 'enlightened' person tells us to stay in the present moment. It's the only moment that exists. It's the only moment that matters," I told him. I felt wise, being able to share some philosophy with a man so much more wiser and mature than me.

He smiled and walked closer. He set down the large jug he held in his hands and grabbed my hands.

"I love being in this present moment with you, Claire," he said, kissing me softly on my forehead. Then, he brushed my cheek with his hand, picked up the jug, and headed back to work.

He didn't say another word, but the whole encounter left a funny feeling in the pit of my stomach. I tried to push the conversation out of my mind. I didn't want to think about it. I didn't ever want to think about not being with Benjamin again.

CHAPTER 14: Hopelessly Devoted To Benjamin

The weeks had past and I truly don't think I'd ever been that happy. The full moon was just two days away, and the others were getting really antsy to get home. Jacquelyn had been discussing the story they planned on telling their families and the authorities. I didn't know if David and Jon would go along with it, but it really didn't matter. Nobody in their right mind would believe that they'd been captured by pirates.

That evening, Benjamin seemed more tense than usual. I could tell that something was on his mind. The thought left that same strange sensation in the pit of my stomach.

"Claire," he whispered, as we walked hand in hand on the deck examining the stars. My heart dropped. I could tell by his tone that something awful was coming.

"You know that I love you, more than anything in this entire world." He paused to look at me. I simply looked up at him, waiting for him to continue.

"When I brought you back to Trenton, you have no idea how hard that was for me. I would give anything to be able to be with you. To have you with me all the time. To have a life with you, a family even.." He stopped. We had never discussed children, so it seemed odd for him to bring that up now. But obviously, it's something he had thought about. I hadn't thought about it at all.

"I'm open to having children," I replied, assuming maybe that's what a large part of this was about. He simply smiled.

"I would love that," he said, grabbing my waist and pulling me in closer. "But a pirate ship is no place for a family. It's no place for you," he said solemnly.

Is he serious? I thought. I could feel my face turning red from the rage. *After everything I'd been through.. Was he still intending to leave me?*

"Benjamin," I started, trying to sound calm. "We've been through this before. The last time you left me, I literally died inside. Look at all I've been through just to get back to you! There is no way that I could ever survive that again. Do you understand? My heart is with you, and that's where I want to be. It's where I want to stay."

"I cannot allow you to throw your life away, Claire," he replied. I could tell that he'd actually put some thought into his asinine position.

"How am I throwing my life away if I'm *choosing* to spend it with you?" I rebutted. "I should have a choice in this." I hung my head.

"This ship is absolutely miserable and you'd be miserable in six months or less," Benjamin countered.

"So then, if I feel cooped up or bored, or miserable, I'll just get off on the full moon when you dock us. I'll walk around, maybe grab something to eat. Do some shopping. And then I'll come right back to be with you," I insisted. I grabbed his hand.

He held my hand and smiled.

"I love how devoted you are to me," he simply said. "But I won't let you waste your life."

"It's *my* life to waste!" I shouted. I was starting to lose my patience. There was no way that I was leaving Benjamin again. "After everything I went through to find you..." I started weeping.

He held me close. I buried my head in his shoulder. "I know," he said, after a long while.

I begged and pleaded with Benjamin, but it was no use. His mind was made up. He refused to allow me to waste my life on that ship, as he put it.

I cried for what seemed like hours. I didn't know how much longer I had to be with him. Benjamin held me, kissed my forehead from time to time, and played with my hair. Eventually, I was exhausted from sobbing, so he picked me up and gently brought me to his room and placed me on the bed. I don't remember falling asleep that night.

CHAPTER 15: My Heart Is Numb

When I woke the next morning, my eyes were red and puffy from hours of tears. My throat was sore and my voice was hoarse. But I was feeling surprisingly optimistic, for I had a new plan.

I rolled over to Benjamin already awake. He kissed my lips. "Good morning," he said. I smiled back.

"I'm going to find a different way to break the curse," I told him. He didn't so much as budge. "There has to be something that somebody can do.. Maybe a different witch?" I suggested. He lay still, not moving.

"Do you think I haven't tried that?" he finally spoke. "What do you think I did the whole time we were apart?"

"But you can't leave the ship," I countered. "So, you only have Genevieve to help you. I can go to shore. I can read books, and go online, I can even go to a different town if need be," I tried to sound convincing. I knew Benjamin wouldn't understand what "online" meant. My voice was getting raspier by the sentence.

"Let me get you something for your throat," Benjamin said sweetly. I nodded in agreement. He left and came back about twenty minutes later with an awful tasting tea. I quickly swallowed it. Healing was Genevieve's expertise and I expected for my throat to start feeling better instantly. It did begin to feel a little numb. Unfortunately, so did the rest of me.

I tried to open my mouth to ask Benjamin if that was normal, but my mouth wouldn't move. I was no longer in control of my eye-lids. They slowly closed, as I tried with all my strength to open them. As they were closing, Benjamin cradled my face. He had a look of anguish on his own.

The last thing I felt were Benjamin's lips on mine.

CHAPTER 16: How Could He?

I woke up to the sound of seagulls pecking at their morning meal. The sun was hot, but there was a familiar breeze that fanned my face. I was sprawled across the sandy beach about fifty feet from the shore.

How could he? It was all I could muster to think. My thoughts were jumbled, as were my feelings. I felt betrayed, angry, and sad.

I felt the panic start to set in and I tried taking slow, deep breaths. *It's going to be okay*, I told myself over and over. I wasn't lying. I'd been through this before, and although it nearly killed me, I'd survived. I could do it again. And this time, I had a plan. I was going to find a different way for the curse to be broken. No matter what it took; I was determined to find a way. And I would not stop until I did.